The Very Best
Teacher

Written by Ye Shil Kim
Illustrated by Mique Moriuchi

sourcebooks
jabberwocky

a b c d e f g h i j k l m

In Ms. Tulip's class there were ten mice.
Rustle, rustle! Squeak, squeak!
Wriggle, wriggle! Squeak, squeak!

Playful Mouse came running in. "I heard the teachers talking in the hallway. Tomorrow is Ms. Tulip's birthday!"
The ten mice decided to have a surprise party for their teacher.

They gathered on the
playground to plan
the birthday party.

What about this?
What about that?
Bustle, bustle! Squeak, squeak!

Frisky Mouse said to the others,
"If you have a good idea, please
raise your tail and speak."

Happy Mouse's tail went up. "Let's have candles on a cake."

Cheerful Mouse's tail went up. "Let's sing a song."

Funny Mouse's tail went up. "Let's give her a present."

"Those are all good ideas," said Frisky
Mouse. "A cake, a song, and a present.
Now, what present would she like?"

Happy Mouse's tail went up. "Something tasty to eat!"

Cheerful Mouse's tail went up. "A poem to read to Ms. Tulip!"

Funny Mouse's tail went up. "A pretty dress for Ms. Tulip."

Star Mouse's tail went up.
"How about a pretty star?"

Silly Mouse's
tail went up.
"Let's give her a
mouse robot!"

Dizzy Mouse's
tail went up.
"We could
write Ms. Tulip
a letter."

They thought about each present.
"We already have a cake, so it can't be food."
"A poem is nice, but she might not remember it."

"We don't have money to buy her fancy clothes."
"A pretty star! But we are her stars. He-he!"
"Miss Tulip's too old to play with a robot mouse."

Scribble,
scribble!

Squeak,
squeak!

The next morning, candles were lit
on the cake and the students shouted,
"Surprise!"
"Happy birthday, Ms. Tulip. Here's a
song and a present for you!"

Ms. Tulip, you are very nice.
I will try not to play around
so much during class.
PLAYFUL MOUSE

When I get nervous I look at you,
Ms. Tulip, and I feel better.
JUMPY MOUSE

Ms. Tulip, I like you best
in the world. But don't
tell my mom and dad.
HELPFUL MOUSE

I like you better than cookies.

Please save me some of your cake.

HAPPY MOUSE

Happy birthday. I hope you know
how much our class loves you.
FRISKY MOUSE

Ms. Tulip, I'll give you a star
for your next birthday.
STAR MOUSE

Dear Ms. Tulip, I'm glad I
get to be In your class.
CHEERFUL MOUSE

Ms. Tulip, I like you so much.
I also like your new glasses.
FUNNY MOUSE

From now on I'll go to bed
early and be a good mouse.
DIZZY MOUSE

Ms. Tulip, I like robots.
Do you like robots?
SILLY MOUSE

Ms. Tulip was very happy. "Oh, class! Thank you so much! You surprised me with a cake and your song, but I like your letter most of all. I will never forget this wonderful party. You are the best students a teacher could ever have."

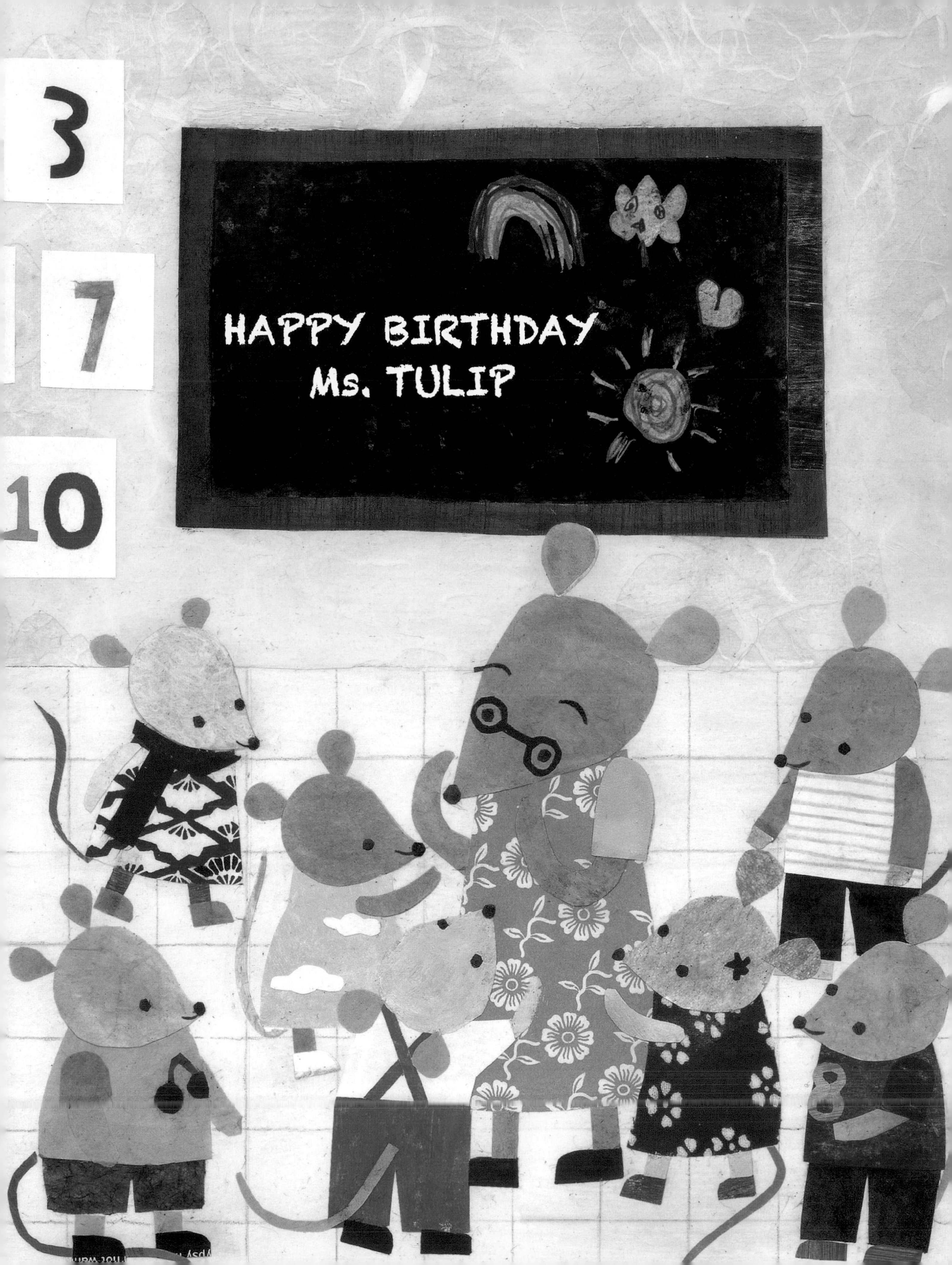
3
7
10
HAPPY BIRTHDAY
Ms. TULIP

The Very Best Teacher
Written by Ye Shil Kim
Illustrated by Mique Moriuchi
Edited by Joy Crowley
Sourcebooks Jabberwocky

Originally published as 선생님 사랑해요 (We Love You Teacher), © Aram Publishing, 2008.

Published by Sourcebooks Jabberwocky, an imprint of Sourcebooks, Inc.
P.O. Box 4410, Naperville, Illinois 60567-4410
(630) 961-3900
Fax: (630) 961-2168
www.jabberwockykids.com

Originally published in 2008 in Korea by Aram Publishing.
Library of Congress Cataloging-in-Publication data is on file with the publisher.

Source of Production: Leo Paper, Heshan City, Guangdong Province, China
Date of Production: March 2015
Run Number: 5003418
Printed and bound in China.
LEO 10 9 8 7 6 5 4 3 2 1